What do the grown-ups do?

Papa the Stockfarmer

"Utterly charming, full of facts and a great career guide."
Tony Boullemier, author of The Little Book of Monarchs.

" An informative and fun way to introduce your children to the world of living."
Gordon Buchanan, Wildlife film maker
(BBC Springwatch, Autumnwatch, The Polar Bear Family and Me).

"What a refreshing and innovative way of introducing children to career possibilities in later life. A delightful series of books which gently guides younger children through the adult world of work. The accompanying photographs of the main characters bring the lives of Joe the Fisherman, Fiona the Doctor and Papa the Stock Farmer, to life."
Louise White, Broadcaster.

"Really detailed and informative books, which contain exactly the questions that intelligent children ask, and adults are often unable to answer. There is fun, humour and a wonderful sense of place too."
Dr Ken Greig, Rector, Hutchesons' Grammar School.

"As an educator in the US there is more and more stress placed upon children being able to access non-fiction writing. Within her books, Mairi McLellan has done something many children's authors are unable to do: she has created non-fiction books that are compelling and highly readable. May all of children's non-fiction literature begin to engage students as McLellan's books do. If this is a new trend in children's books, teachers across the US would be so grateful."
Marlene Moyer, 5th & 6th Grade teacher, Nevada, USA.

Matador
9 Priory Business Park
Kibworth Beauchamp
Leicestershire LE8 0RX, UK
Tel: (+44) 116 279 2299
Fax: (+44) 116 279 2277
Email: books@troubador.co.uk
Web: www.troubador.co.uk/matador

ISBN: 978 1783061 198

British Library Cataloguing in Publication Data.
A catalogue record for this book is available from the British Library.

Matador is an imprint of Troubador Publishing Ltd

www.kidseducationalbooks.com

What do the grown-ups do?

Papa the Stockfarmer

Mairi McLellan

What do the grown-ups do?

Dear reader,

What do the grown-ups do? is a series of books designed to educate children about the workplace in a light-hearted and interesting manner. The ideal age range is five to ten years and the feedback from the children has been superb. They seem to have a genuine interest in learning about the workplace, keen to understand what the grown-ups do all day.

The objective is to offer the children an insight into adult working life, to stimulate their thinking and to help motivate them to learn more about the jobs that interest them. Perhaps by introducing these concepts early, we can broaden their ideas for the future they have ahead of them as well as increase their awareness of the work of those around them. It's just a start and at this age, although the message is serious, it is designed to be fun.

For younger children who will be doing a combination of reading and 'being read to', this book will be reasonably challenging. I have deliberately tried not to over-simplify the books too much to maintain reality, whilst making them fun to enjoy.

You can read the books in any order but they are probably best starting from the beginning. The order of the series can be found at the back of this book.

Many more will be coming soon so please check the website for updates www.kidseducationalbooks.com.

I hope you enjoy them.

Happy reading,

Mairi

A note of thanks to my wonderful family, Grahams and McLellans, and to Weesie for her grammar assistance! Also to Donald and Alec for all their help with the cattle, the fencing and the silage in the middle of winter. Most importantly, a very special thanks to Granny and Papa for the Highland cattle and for the opportunity to live in such a beautiful part of the world.

Viva Badaneel.

Life by the sea in Badaneel

Ava, Skye and Gracie Mackenzie lived by the sea in a pretty little village called Badaneel in the northwest Highlands. It was one of the most beautiful places in Scotland with big sandy beaches, tall mountains and fantastic views over to the Outer Isles.

Views around Badaneel.

In the village, little white houses lay scattered along the shoreline with a cosy café overlooking the sea and an assortment of boats anchored in the shelter of the harbour.

Badaneel bay at sunrise.

The girls were almost all the same age. The twins, Ava and Skye, were five and Gracie was only just over a year younger at four years old. Being almost the same height, with the same blondish, unruly long hair, they looked like triplets and most people got them muddled up!

It was the summer holidays and no-one wanted to leave Badaneel at this time of year because there was so much fun to be had, playing in the sea and roaming the hills. Being situated so far north, Badaneel hardly got dark in the summer months. The opposite was true in winter when it was pitch black around four o'clock, so everyone had to make the most of summer while they could.

One of the children's favourite past-times in Badaneel was looking for the animals. There was wildlife everywhere you looked. Seals and dolphins were plentiful in the bay as well as lots of different birds such as golden eagles, sea-eagles, herons, seagulls and gannets. Sammy the seal was always sunbathing on the rock to the east of Badaneel. He was an easy find!

Sammy the seal in his favourite sunbathing spot by the east entrance to Badaneel.

Barney the donkey.

In the hills and mountains, the girls went for long walks to find the different animals.

One of their favourites was Barney the donkey. Ava, Skye and Gracie carried carrots in their pockets so they could give him a treat when they saw him. He did not like celery!

New born lambs in the field.

Springtime was especially exciting as it meant the arrival of the lambs which were unbelievably cute!

Most of the sheep in Badaneel were Blackface sheep as they are one of the hardiest of breeds, better suited to survive the harsh weather and poorer pastures of the Highlands.

A stag with big antlers grazing in the paddock.

If they were very quiet, they sometimes saw deer grazing. Red deer roam in large numbers around the hills and mountains of Badaneel, heading down to the lower slopes to rut (mate) and out-winter.

Some deer are shot for sporting purposes, although the venison is always eaten so it does not go to waste. Stags (male deer) are measured on their size and number of points on their antlers. Any stag with six points on each antler is described as a 'Royal'. Today, the stalking of deer is based on the welfare of the herd as well as their impact on the surrounding countryside. It is no longer acceptable to trophy hunt healthy stags with the largest antlers. Instead, stalkers cull the weaker animals in an effort to maintain a healthy herd.

There is controversy as to whether the deer should be culled at all and some groups think a fifty percent cull is needed whilst others think none is required. Most groups maintain that it is a good idea to cull the weaker or sick animals.

A cattle grid across the road.

During their wanders, the girls learned about cattle grids which were bars of metal across the road. They were attached on either side to a long fence. The cattle grids made a funny noise when you drove over them. Ava, Skye and Gracie thought it sounded just like a rude noise from someone's bottom and they giggled every time Mother drove across them!

The cattle grids were used to manage the animals in Badaneel. They kept the deer away from the new trees that had been planted, otherwise the deer would eat them all! They also helped to keep the local cows that wandered freely in the summer from straying too far from home and getting lost.

Jobs

The Mackenzie girls loved playing but they also had work to do. Their parents said that everyone had to work and that if you did a good day's work, you enjoyed your playtime even more!

The girls got pocket money for their work to buy themselves treats so it was quite a good arrangement. They had lots of different jobs including:

- Washing the car
- Gathering the logs
- Feeding the dog
- Sweeping the floors
- Peeling the vegetables
- Picking the herbs and vegetables from the garden
- Washing the paintwork
- Tidying their bedroom
- Vacuum cleaning
- and so on…

Ava, Skye and Gracie were good workers and although there was never a shortage of jobs to be done in the house and around the garden, they were always much more interested in what the grown-ups did!

The adults seemed so busy and they didn't understand why they had to work so much. They also seemed to earn much more pocket money for their work, which was all very confusing.

Mother had promised to show them the 'grown-up jobs' and last week they had met Joe the Fisherman to learn about creel fishing. Mother said that it was important to understand about lots of different jobs before deciding what to do when you are grown-up.

She said that one of the most important things is to find a job that you enjoy doing. They wondered what job would be next.

Ava, Skye and Gracie were busy watering the vegetables in the garden when their Mother called over.

"Girls! It's Papa on the phone! He needs some help moving his cows. Papa can show you how to be a farmer! Hurry, hurry!" she shouted.

The girls looked at each other. They had helped move sheep before but they had never worked with the cows!

"Yikes!" said Ava. "Those things have horns!" she exclaimed.

Papa

Papa was a very clever man and a hard worker. He was the children's grandfather and Mother's father. Mother said that Papa could get most people out of any problem because he thought in a different way to everyone else.

He was also extremely strong. Mother said he had hands like 'mole-grips', which were a special tool used to grip things really hard!

Papa was great at telling stories, with an infectious laugh that made those around him laugh too.

His parents and grandparents were also from Badaneel and they had been farmers and fishermen a very long time ago. When he was growing up, Papa spent as much time as he could working on farms and fishing boats. He had done lots of different jobs in his life but one of his favourite jobs was working on the farm and his favourite cattle were the Highlanders!

He was most happy when he was either walking the hills or out on the sea.

Papa out fishing with the girls.

Papa gives Ava a carry!

Papa walking up the hill with the Highland cows and his sheepdog.

 8

The children had watched Papa's cows many times before from over the fence. They thought they were the prettiest cows they had ever seen, with long woolly coats and big sweeping horns. The calves were the cutest. Ava thought they looked even cuddlier than her teddy bears.

They ran up the garden and headed off with Mother to find Papa.

"So is Papa a farmer, Mama?" asked Ava.

"Indeed he is, darling," replied Mother, "There are lots of different types of farmers, such as arable farmers who grow cereals

The girls with Father, looking at the cattle.

Highland calves, about two months old.

like wheat, oats and barley. There are pig farmers, deer farmers, hen farmers, potato farmers, pea farmers and many others but Papa is a stock farmer. Papa breeds cows and sheep to sell them for their beef and lamb. When we have a roast beef dinner, it is often from one of Papa's cows."

"Oh, what a shame, poor cows!" shrieked Skye.

"I know it seems harsh but the cattle and sheep have a very good life here on the hill. They are here because people need food but they also play a very important role in nature conservation management, especially when grazed at low density like they are here. Papa will tell you more about it if you ask him," she smiled.

"Hmmmm." The girls weren't sure. They really liked roast beef and lamb but it did seem rather unfair to kill these beautiful animals.

A Highland cow in the paddock.

Highland calf on the hill.

"Girls, life is not perfect. We grow vegetables and we eat them; we rear cattle or sheep and we eat them. People rear pigs and sell them for bacon or ham. It's just part of life. Besides, when you learn more about managing the land you will see the benefits they bring to other insects, animals and plant life," she smiled.

As they arrived at the gate they saw the cows stampeding over the brow of the hill with Papa coming up behind them. They were massive animals and although they were cute, they also looked quite scary!

The Highland cows charging over the hill.

"Are we going to have to go near them, Mama?" asked Gracie.

"The grown-ups will be nearest but you can help too," smiled Mother. "You are still a bit small to be up against a cow, but you're old enough to start learning what farmers do," she said.

Papa's Highland bulls, Sean and Calum.

The cows arrived at the gate with Papa, who was carrying his shepherd's stick. He looked completely calm amongst the chaos.

"Morning girls! Have you come to help me?" he asked.

"Hi Papa! Yes, Mama says we are a bit young but that we need to start learning about farming."

"No time like the present," laughed Papa. "We'll make little farmers of you yet! Today we need to move the cattle so I'd be very glad to have a hand!"

"Mama says that you are a stock farmer. Is that right, Papa?" asked Ava.

"Indeed I am," smiled Papa. "Stock just means 'animals' and we have Highland cattle and Blackface sheep on this farm. We have different things on other farms further south because the land is different."

"How is the land different?" asked Gracie.

"In simple terms, the type of farming you do changes depending on whether you have *high ground* or *low ground*.

High ground in the Highlands with lots of heather.

Lower ground with better grass.

"On farms with lower, richer ground we keep different types of cattle such as Aberdeen Angus and Shorthorn cattle as well as different types of sheep such as Texels and Suffolks. Typically, the lower ground animals are bigger, faster growing breeds. For example, we have pedigree Texels, which grow faster but also require more management, better conditions and better feeding than the hill sheep."

Ava and Skye help to herd the lowland sheep.

Pedigree Texel sheep.

The Highlands

"What type of land do we have here?" asked Ava.

"Up here in the Highlands where we are on high ground, the soil is generally of poor quality and not many animals can survive on these pastures. However, the Highland cow is very good at living here and so is the Blackie sheep. They love to roam around the heather in the mountains!" said Papa.

Papa's Highland cow in the paddock.

A Blackface or 'Blackie' sheep.

"Did you know that Highland cattle are one of the oldest native breeds in Scotland? They are beautiful animals but although they are pretty to look at, they are also one of the hardiest of breeds. They are one of the only types of cattle that can thrive on these rough hills in the bad weather. They are also very good for the land and will improve the ground."

"How do they improve the ground?" said Ava.

"Well," said Papa, "it all probably sounds rather disgusting to you, but they dung or 'poo' everywhere on the hill. This dung is great for the ground and encourages lots of beetles and other insects, which helps all sorts of things like the grass, the birds and even the fish in the river!"

"How on earth does the poo help fish in the river?" chuckled Gracie.

"It's a process which happens over time. Did you know that each Highland cow generates one quarter of its bodyweight in insect life every year? That means about 125 kilograms of insects – about six times more than you weigh! All these little insects filter into the rivers and feed the fish. They also feed the birds. Everything is connected. They call it the food chain," he explained.

Papa's Highland cows.

"Where are we in the food chain?" asked Skye.

"Apparently at the top, although not always! If you met a lion in Africa I think you might find yourself underneath him in the food chain!" laughed Papa.

"The cattle create a food chain for other animals and insects but they are also part of it," explained Papa.

"Like when we eat roast beef for dinner?" said Ava.

"Just like that, yes," smiled Papa.

Papa looking for new calves that need their ears tagged to identify them.

"Do the cattle stay out on the hill all year?" asked Skye.

"The Highland cattle have very woolly coats which keep them nice and warm. Their coat has two layers; an outer layer of long hair which lets the rain run off and a shorter woolly layer underneath to keep them cosy.

They stay on the hill all year round except for calving when I bring them down to the paddock to keep an eye on them. They get almost everything they need to eat from the hill, although I do give them a few extra special treats to make sure they get all the vitamins and minerals that they need to stay strong and healthy. They even go down to the sea to have a chew at the seaweed to get extra minerals. I can tell you it gives some of the people on the boats a fright when they see a Highland down on the shore beside them!" laughed Papa.

"In winter we bring in some silage to give them a little bit extra as there is not as much food for them on the hill in the winter months," he said.

A Highland cow and her new calf beside the silage in the paddock.

"What is silage?" asked Gracie.

"Silage is basically a way of preserving the good grass we have in the summer so that we can use it in the winter," explained Papa.

The silage bales ready to be wrapped in the field.

The tractor with its baling machine attached.

Ava and Skye playing in the tractor.

"To make silage, we cut the grass and all the other plants that are growing amongst it when it contains its highest nutrient levels. It is then allowed to dry a little in the field. A tractor with a special machine called a 'baler' drives up and down the field to pick up the grass and make it into 'bales'. The bales are like big sausage shapes and are tied with string before being wrapped in plastic to keep the air out.

Gracie jumping off the hay bales.   Skye jumping off the hay bales.

"If a bale gets pierced, it must be used immediately otherwise it will go mouldy and won't be any good for the animals.

If the grass that is cut is left for longer to dry, it becomes *haylage*. If it is left until it is almost dry, it becomes *hay*. Haylage is wrapped in bales but hay tends to be left unwrapped.

It all sounds a little complicated and, to be honest, sometimes it can be but it is a great way to feed the cattle when there is no grass on the ground," said Papa.

"Phew!" sighed Gracie. "That does sound very complicated!"

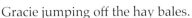 19

"There is a lot of science involved to get the right grasses growing in the right soil," said Papa. "It is very important to make good quality silage so that the cattle get all the right vitamins. However, once you have these things sorted, the process is not so difficult assuming you get the right weather! That's why you see so many balers working really late at night because they need to get the bales wrapped at the right time of the year with the right weather. They work very hard at baling time."

The silage is wrapped and stored outside.

"Is silage the only thing that the cows eat in the winter?" asked Gracie.

"Up here in the Highlands the cattle eat silage in the winter as well as some tasty 'cobbs', which are dried pellets of food and mineral 'licks'. Each of these contain lots of different vitamins and minerals to keep them healthy. Whilst we must ensure that they get all the nutrients they need, we must also ensure that they don't get fat otherwise it makes it harder for them to calve," explained Papa.

"On the farms that are on lower ground, we also plough the land and grow crops such as barley and oats. The grain is used for feeding the animals and the straw that comes from the crop is used to make cosy beds for those cattle that need to be inside during the winter. Barley makes good bedding straw and oats make good eating straw," he said.

"Why don't you give them silage all year round? That way you'd know they had plenty to eat?" asked Skye.

"That is a very good question, Skye and I'll tell you why. The reason is that if the cows get too used to being fed by us, then they don't go and graze to look for food themselves. They become dependent on man and that is not good. Besides, we couldn't afford to feed them silage all year round! Just like any business, you have to watch your costs if you want to make money, and farming is certainly no different."

"Why are you taking them off the hill today, Papa?" asked Ava.

"We are taking them to get their TB test. TB stands for tuberculosis, or specifically bovine tuberculosis (bTB), which is the one that affects cattle. The disease attacks the lungs and can eventually lead to death. There is a great deal of debate surrounding bTB and the way it is transmitted. It is believed to be primarily passed from one animal to another by breathing in bacteria. bTB can be passed to humans but instances of this are rare! The vet is coming to do special tests on the animals over the next few days."

"Do you think they have TB, Papa?" asked Ava.

"No, it is very unlikely. Our area is TB free but it is always best to check. We need to walk the cows down the road to the paddock. I've set up a pen in the paddock ready for them to go straight into."

"Is it going to be easy to walk them down?" asked Skye.

"I think with all the help we've got we shouldn't have too many problems. The most important thing to remember when you are dealing with the cattle is that you mustn't look frightened! If they think you are scared they won't do as they are told and you get yourself into problems. The other thing to remember is not to get stuck between a cow and her calf. That can be really dangerous so it is best to stay away from the calves," said Papa rather seriously.

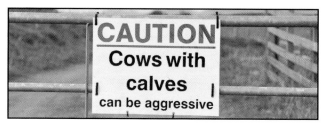

A sign to warn the walkers.

The girls thought that looking brave was easier said than done but they headed down the road with Papa. Papa was at the front with a bag of tasty feed to tempt them along. Father, Mother and the girls were behind the cattle and the girls had little sticks to wave at the cows in case they decided to go the wrong way. It was all going fine. The cars on the single-track road caused a little bit of a problem from time to time because they scared the cows. Sometimes the cows wandered off the road to eat some tasty grass but Papa ran around them and got them back on track. Soon they were at the paddock with the cows in the pen.

"Well that was fairly easy!" said Papa. "It must have been all your help! Thank you girls!"

The cattle in a pen ready for the vet to come.

Suddenly the vet appeared. "We have a problem. One of these cows has just calved and according to your records, you are one calf short which means…"

"Oh no! We have a new born calf still up the hill somewhere!" bellowed Papa.

"Indeed," responded the vet rather solemnly.

"There was me thinking it had been an easy trip," sighed Papa. "Now I'm going to have to go back up the hill to try to find the missing calf. The chances of that happening are very slim."

"Why don't you think you'll be able to find it, Papa?" asked the girls.

"Well you see, the cows tend to hide their calves. When they are born they are very little and they curl up into a tiny ball under a tree or something. It is impossible to find them. It's like looking for a needle in a haystack!"

"We'll help you Papa. Can we Mama?" asked the girls.

"Of course you can! We'll all go!" said Mother.

They looked and looked over every hill and glen. It was a big rough area of about 200 acres with lots of heather and trees and so many places to hide!

The Mackenzie girls set off with Father to look for the missing calf!

Father can't see it anywhere!

"No, this is not going to work," puffed Papa after two hours of walking around.

"So how are you going to find the calf?" asked Skye.

"We're not. The calf does not want to be found by us. He wants his mother and so the only solution is to get the mother back up the hill to let her find the calf."

And so they went back to the pen, manoeuvred the mother cow out, which was rather tricky, and walked her back up the road onto the hill.

"We'll have to leave her until tomorrow," said Papa. "She's obviously quite flustered with all this moving about as well as being taken away from her new born calf. I'll come back first thing in the morning to see if she's found him."

The following day the girls went back to help Papa. After another two hours of searching on the hill they finally found both the calf and its mother.

"Thank goodness!" exclaimed Papa. "What a lovely sight! I was worried that the calf might be dead but he seems fine. Right then, we need to get these two back down to the paddock!"

The Highland cow with her new born calf, safe and sound on the hill.

It was a big fiasco moving them off the hill, as the mother cow was clearly upset by all the fuss. They had to get them into the back of the trailer, as the baby calf was too little to walk all the way down the road. The cow was not keen to get into the trailer and was getting very angry. At one point, Mother thought that the cow was going to charge at her, and she got so frightened that she leapt over the fence backwards!

Mother seemed rather embarrassed after she picked herself off the ground. "Sorry Dad," she said. "I thought she was going to go for me!"

"It's ok," said Papa to Mother. "Cattle can be very dangerous and if in doubt, it's best just to get out the way if they are angry!"

Soon enough, all the cows were back in the paddock. Papa, Mother, Father and the girls went over to inspect the little calf when it was lying down. It didn't look too happy.

The little calf looks unwell.

Father picked it up to inspect it and noticed he had blood on his hands!

"Where is this blood coming from?" he asked, looking rather confused.

Papa turned the calf over to have a look. The whole side of the calf was covered in maggots!

"YUUUUUUUUK!" cried the girls.

It truly was disgusting. The maggots were swarming all over the entire side of the calf. The poor little thing must have been in agony!

"Oh my goodness!" exclaimed Papa. "This is not good. Not good at all. We are lucky we found this calf otherwise it would have been dead by tomorrow."

"Can we save it?" asked Gracie.

"Maybe. We'll give it our best shot," replied Papa, looking rather serious.

Papa went over to his pick-up truck and brought back some medicine. It was used for getting rid of ticks, lice and other unpleasant creatures. He administered double quantities because the calf was in such a bad state.

"Watch this," said Papa as he poured the liquid onto the calf's back. "The maggots will pour out like a river. They hate this stuff! With any luck, they have not got inside the calf to damage his organs. We may have got to him just in the nick of time," he said.

They all watched. Sure enough, after a couple of minutes all the maggots started pouring out.

"Gross!" squirmed Ava.

Everyone nodded. It was absolutely disgusting but the medicine seemed to be working. At that point, the vet arrived to inspect the situation. He had a quick look and gave the calf a Vitamin E injection and some antibiotics.

"He may be fine, he may not," he said sternly. "We've done all we can, so just keep an eye on him. He's a lucky little fellow that we were gathering them up today."

"How did he get the maggots?" asked Ava.

"Well this calf should have been born with the rest in spring but instead he was born in August when there are lots of flies about," said Papa. "The Highland calves have deep, fluffy hair and the flies get attracted to a bit of dung or blood and lay their eggs in the fluffy coats. These eggs become the maggots you saw today. They are unpleasant little creatures aren't they?"

Everyone nodded again. The calf had to be left in peace to recover and there was still work to be done with the rest of the cattle. Back over at the pen they soon finished the TB testing. The vet looked pleased.

"Everything seems fine," he said. "I'll be back in a couple of days to finish the testing. Your animals look healthy and all seems well. In the meantime, all you can do is keep an eye on that little calf and hope that the maggots haven't got in too deep," he said.

"Indeed I will," said Papa.

It was past dinner time and everyone was exhausted. Papa came home with them for a meal and they sat chatting around the big farmhouse table.

"What is your favourite part of being a farmer, Papa?" asked Skye.

"My favourite part is working with the animals. You have to like animals to be a farmer! I also love working in the countryside and being in the fresh air."

"What is the worst part of being a farmer?" asked Ava.

"The worst part is when the animals get sick, like today. I find it very sad when they suffer and even worse when they die."

"Do the cows get ill often, Papa?" asked Gracie.

"Not very often but you need to look after them to keep them well. There are lots of different things you need to learn about animal disease and how to prevent it. The animals are blood tested once a year to ensure they are in the best possible health. The cattle and sheep are regularly dosed with medicine to stop them getting lice, worms, ticks, maggots and other unpleasant things!

We use a 'cattle handling system' which is a group of gates and pens joined together with a 'race' to get them in a single line and a 'crush' to hold them still while we give them jags, blood-tests or anything else we need to do," explained Papa. "The handling system makes it much easier to manage the cattle and help keep them in good health. The main cattle diseases we look out for include:

- BVD (Bovine Virus Diarrhoea)
- IBR (Infectious Bovine Rhinotracheitis)
- Johne's disease
- TB
- Mastitis
- Pneumonia

There are many others and it is important to keep a close eye on your stock and check them regularly to make sure they are ok," he explained.

The girls playing in the cattle handling.

The 'race' to get the cattle into a single line.

The Blackface sheep in a pen.

"Calving is a busy time of year because we need to check the cattle all the time to make sure there are no calving problems. Assuming the calf arrives safely, we need to make sure that the calf is getting milk from its mother. The first milk that the mother produces after her calf is born is called 'colostrum'. It's not too disimilar to humans when babies get their milk from their mother," smiled Papa. "Colostrum contains less lactose (sugar) but more protein, vitamins and minerals than normal milk. It also contains *immunoglobulins,* which is a very big word isn't it?" laughed Papa.

The girls laughed too and got their tongues completely tied trying to repeat it!

"Immunoglobulins are antibodies that stop calves getting sick. It is extremely important that the calf receives at least two litres of colostrum within the first six hours of birth as the antibodies in colostrum help protect the calf from disease.

We try everything we can to ensure that the calves get this colostrum but in some unfortunate cases where the mother cow dies or cannot feed her calf, we have to try to make a substitute and bottle feed the calves until they can look after themselves. It can be very time consuming but well worth it when you see a healthy calf skipping around the hill!" he smiled.

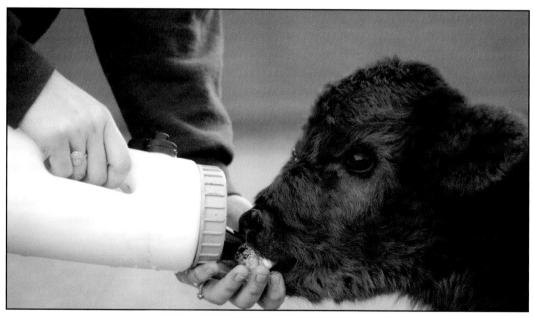

A calf whose mother died gets a feed from a bottle.

"How do you become a farmer?" asked Gracie.

"There are lots of ways to farm," said Papa. "If you are interested in farming, it's a good idea to find a farm nearby where you can learn how to use farm machinery and how to handle the animals.

Otherwise, the main ways to become a farmer are:

- To be brought-up on a farm.
- To go to Agricultural College and then get a job on a farm.
- To go straight from school into a work apprenticeship.

Papa and Ava round up the sheep with Lass the sheepdog.

Papa leads a one year old to the show.

How do you make money from farming, Papa?" asked Ava.

"We make money by selling stock to other farmers who buy our prize animals for breeding.

We also make money by selling animals as premium beef or lamb to butchers, farmers markets, supermarkets and top class restuarants," he replied.

"In both cases, you get a higher price for your cattle if you have better quality animals."

They finished dinner and Papa headed off home, promising to phone with an update on the calf.

"Farming is more complicated than I thought," said Ava.

"It certainly is!" laughed Mother. "Farmers have to have knowledge of a lot of things to manage the farm. They have to understand animal health, grassland management, soil composition, nutrition for the animals and so on, as well as know how to handle the cows, which is a challenge in itself!" she explained.

"They also have to learn how to operate machinery such as tractors and all the different tools that go with them. Then they need to know about mechanics so that they can fix them when they break down. Farming is much more complicated than most people think," she smiled.

The tractor takes a 'calf creep' up the hill for feeding.

The calf creep ready to feed the calves in winter.

Lots of different tractor attachments. Each one does a different job.

"I like animals and I like being outside," said Ava. "I think I would like to be a farmer."

"It is great being outside on days like this when the sun is shining," said Mother. "However, in the middle of winter when it's cold and raining, it is definitely less fun! There is also a great deal of paperwork to do.

If you decide to do a job, you need to understand all the good and bad aspects of it because unfortunately we can't just pick and choose the bits we like in work," she explained.

It had been a busy day and although the maggots had been unbelievably disgusting, the girls had really enjoyed their time being a farmer.

They went to bed thinking about the calf and hoping it would be alright.

The following morning Papa phoned.

"Good news!" he exclaimed. "The calf is up on its feet and walking about! I think he is going to be fine and I expect to see him running around the field in the next few days with all the other calves. Thank you for your help. We have called him 'Lucky' because he is indeed very, very lucky!" he laughed.

'Lucky' is up on his feet and happy in the paddock.

"Well done girls!" said Mother. "You helped save a calf and that is a great achievement. Farming is a tough but very rewarding job and you have all done very well today. Since you have been working so hard, I think it is time for you to go and play as you definitely deserve a break!" she laughed.

"Yaaaaay!" they shouted as they rushed off into the garden to play on the zip-wire. That was two jobs they had seen now and they wondered what the next one would be...

Playtime on the zip-wire for Gracie and Ava.

Caught at the bottom because it goes super fast!

The end.

What do the grown-ups do?

The books are available in paperback and e-book and can be purchased through all major bookstores as well as on online. For more information, please check the website:

www.kidseducationalbooks.com

The *What do the grown-ups do?* series in order of publishing:

Book 1: Joe the Fisherman

Book 2: Papa the Stock Farmer

Book 3: Sean the Actor

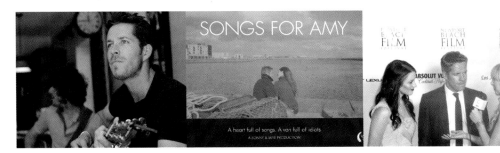

Book 4: Fiona the Doctor

Book 5: Richard the Vet